WARRIOR

ZONE

WARRIOR ZONE

KRISTEN SABERRE

MINNEAPOLIS

Darby Creek
A division of Lerner Publishing Group, Inc.
241 First Avenue North
Minneapolis, MN 55401 USA

For reading levels and more information, look up this title at www.lernerbooks.com.

Cover photograph: wavebreakmedia/Shutterstock.com.

Main body text set in Janson Text LT Std 12/17.5.
Typeface provided by Adobe Systems.

Library of Congress Cataloging-in-Publication Data

Names: SaBerre, Kristen, author.
Title: Warrior Zone / Kristen SaBerre.
Description: Minneapolis : Darby Creek, [2019] | Summary: A finalist on her favorite
    reality television show, nationally ranked teen gymnast Fiona Chu must decide what
    to do after learning that the producers have already chosen the winner.
Identifiers: LCCN 2018004813 (print) | LCCN 2018011804 (ebook) |
    ISBN 9781541541863 (eb pdf) | ISBN 9781541540231 (lb : alk. paper)
Subjects: | CYAC: Reality television programs—Fiction. | Television—Production
    and direction—Fiction. | Competition (Psychology)—Fiction. | Conduct of life—
    Fiction. | Friendship—Fiction.
Classification: LCC PZ7.1.S18 (ebook) | LCC PZ7.1.S18 War 2019 (print) | DDC
    [Fic]—dc23

LC record available at https://lccn.loc.gov/2018004813

Manufactured in the United States of America
1-45228-36610-6/22/2018

For EllaRose and Dot,
my rebel icons

CHAPTER 1

Run, Fiona! A voice in my head is yelling at me, but my legs are refusing to obey. *Run! Run now! Or would you rather be impaled by an eighteen-inch Viking horn?*

I definitely do *not* want that, but that's what will happen if I don't move. *Whoosh.* A long, pointy horn shoots out from the wall a foot in front of me. It lingers for a second, then flies back inside the wall. *Whoosh.* Another one appears so close to my head that I can feel my hair move. Every few seconds, another horn bursts from the tall stone wall at a new location. The longer I stand still, the higher my risk of being struck. I know my best strategy is to run through the twenty feet of hallway as fast as possible and hope for the best. *So why can't I get my legs to move?*

Whoosh. Another horn jabs the air, this time right behind me. As it disappears into the wall, my legs start working again and I instinctively take a step backward to where the horn was a moment before. Something in my gut tells me this horn won't be back right away. The next horn stabs the air five steps ahead of me. When it retracts into the wall, I run as fast as I can into the space it just left. The space left by each horn is a short-term safe zone. "Behind, ahead . . . now what?" I whisper to myself, trying not to freak out. I remember just in time and duck as a horn shoots out above me. "Behind, ahead, above. Okay, Fiona, you can do this."

Sure enough, the next horn shoots out behind me. I back into the space it leaves. The next horn emerges ahead. I sprint into the space it leaves and duck. The horn above comes and goes, and I repeat this process—behind, ahead, above—following the horns, slowly making my way forward.

Finally, I make it out of the stone hallway. Light washes over me, and I see I'm on the deck of a massive ship. But I'm not free yet. This only ends when I make it to the top of the ship's mast and capture its flag. Only then will I know my fate.

Rigging ropes hang over the mast. *They're my way up*, I think. Taking a running leap, I jump as high as I can and reach for the lowest-hanging rope. My hands clutch the rope, but it's slippery. I zoom toward the ground, the rope burning in my hands. I tighten my fists and pray the friction is enough to slow my fall. I jolt to a stop in midair. My legs kick the slick mast, hoping for a foothold, but there isn't one—it's just me and the rope.

I know this climb will take a lot of strength. Luckily, as a nationally ranked gymnast, I have plenty. I swing one arm up higher on the rope. I wind my feet around the rope to create a foothold. I push off from my feet and reach up, hand over hand, and I climb. My hands are blistering. My lungs are screaming. My chest is pounding. But I make it to the top of the mast. I grab the red flag and thrust it into the air.

Suddenly, I'm drowning in noise. Although I'm perched on the top of a ship, the noise is not from waves. It is the roar of a live studio audience—everyone is cheering. Lights rise, and I can see, once again, that I'm in a television studio. The ship, the stone walls, every Viking-themed hazard I just conquered was part of a gigantic obstacle course. I am a contestant on *Warrior Zone*, a popular reality show for teen athletes. At the end of the competition, the winner is named the Ultimate Warrior—and gets the grand prize of thirty thousand dollars.

A rolling ladder appears beside me, and I gratefully climb my way down. At the bottom, television cameras wait for me. Someone yells from behind one, "Fiona, how do you feel? And how do you think you did compared to the other warriors?"

"I'm really proud of my work this round," I say, still catching my breath. "I did my best, and I hope it was good enough to get me to the finals."

The cameras turn away, satisfied. I fold over onto my knees and suck in air. Once I can move again, I head toward a refreshment table. I'm dying for water, but a set hand stops me. Like the other dozen set hands, she's wearing a white shirt, has a towel in her back pocket, and holds a walkie talkie in her hand. "Fiona, we need you at the podium for the ceremony."

"Let me grab some water first."

"Sorry, we need you now. They're ready with the results."

My stomach twists with excitement and dread. My results determine whether I get to advance to the finals or if my chance to become the Ultimate Warrior is over.

She herds me across the sound stage. We pass the artificial Viking ship, which is nothing more than a bunch of pipes drilled together and decorated to look like a ship. We pass the bleachers of cheering audience members, and we come to a large red circle painted on the floor. Five other teenagers stand inside it. Like me, they're wearing helmets, different colored tank tops, and athletic shorts. Like me, they also look completely exhausted.

I join them in the circle and one of them hands me a cold bottle of water. We bump fists, then I snag the bottle from him and immediately guzzle half of it. "You look thirsty. Did you just work out or something?" he says sarcastically.

"Good thing this water's better than your jokes, Ravi," I say between gulps.

Ravi is my closest friend on the show. We met two months ago, when we arrived in Los Angeles as quarterfinalists. All quarterfinalists were the winners of their regional competition. I had the highest score out of everyone competing in the entire northwest region of the United States, where I live. Ravi won in Texas, which is so large it's considered its own region. Even though I made it to quarterfinals, I was terrified. Not only because I was away from home, but also because I was about to spend the next four Saturdays powering through obstacle courses and hoping to score high enough to make semifinals. And if I made semifinals, I'd have to do it all over again to make it to the finals. I also knew that, unlike regionals, the courses would be filmed in front of a live studio audience and eventually aired for millions of people to watch on television. Ravi and I walked in the studio door at the same time, wearing the same nervous look. He told me I seemed as lost as he did, so he was going to follow me and hope for the best. I told him that was a terrible idea. We've been friends ever since.

Even though *Warrior Zone* is a competition and only one person will win, Ravi and I help each other along the way. We each cheer the other on as we run the obstacle course. We give each other tips on how to do better next time. We make sure the other one has a bottle of water after their run.

Of the six of us in semifinals, most of us are friendly toward each other. But one guy, Paul, isn't friendly to anyone. He rarely talks with other contestants, and if he does, it's usually

to say something mean. If there is anyone I
want to lose, it's Paul.

A group of set hands comes through and
gets each of us ready to be on camera. One
takes my helmet and straightens my ponytail.
She wipes the sweat off my forehead with a
towel, then sprays my face with a watery mist.
When this happened after my first quarterfinal
course, I asked why she bothered drying me
off if she was just going to spray me down. She
smiled and explained, "We don't want you to
sweat, we want you to glow. Looks better on
camera." That day I learned that even though
this is an athletic competition, it's first and
foremost a television show. And on any TV
show, the people on screen have to look good.

The lights dim over the studio and
a spotlight lands on me and the other
contestants. An announcer's voice booms over
speakers: "Ladies and Gentleman. The time
has come to learn the results of the *Warrior
Zone* semifinals. You know what this means.
The three warriors that rank highest will go
on to compete in the *Warrior Zone* finals for

a chance to win the coveted title of America's Ultimate Warrior. The three warriors that rank lowest? Well . . . we all know what happens to them."

We contestants certainly know what happens to them. It isn't pretty.

All of us link arms and wish each other luck. All of us except Paul. He looks over at the five of us and snorts, "Luck has nothing to do with it, losers."

The spotlight on us changes to swirling, colorful strobe lights. "In third place, with seven hundred and forty-four points, from Providence, Rhode Island, Paul Pierce!"

The crowd goes wild. I groan internally. The swirling lights settle on Paul who flashes a huge smile and waves at the cameras. He looks so friendly when the cameras are on. Only the other contestants know that he's not really like that in real life.

Paul steps out of the circle and onto one of the three winners' blocks. Now there are only two spots left for finalists. Ravi and I share a nervous look.

"In second place," booms the announcer, "with eight hundred and twelve points, from Austin, Texas, Ravi Murthy!"

The crowd erupts in cheers. I turn to Ravi with wide eyes. We grab arms and jump up and down together. I shove him out of the circle, and he joins Paul on the winners' blocks.

The crowd goes quiet. The only sound I can hear is my heart pounding in my ears. There is only one more winner's block. *Will it be mine?*

Finally, the announcer comes back over the speaker. His next sentence seems to take forever. "In first place, with a record-breaking time of four minutes and seventeen seconds, and a total score of one thousand and thirty points, this year's only female heading into the finals, from Portland, Oregon, the one, the only, Fiona Chu!"

Everything shifts into slow motion. I see faces smiling, hands clapping, and people cheering from all directions. My legs move me out of the circle and onto the tallest winner's block. *I did it! I am going to the finals. I'm one step closer to being a champion.*

"Congratulations to our finalists," the announcer hollers over the excited audience. "Unfortunately our last three warriors didn't make it to the finals. They don't get to leave the circle. They are, say it with me, Looo-serrrs."

The audience chants with him. "Lo-sers, Lo-sers, Lo-sers!" The chanting builds. I watch the three contestants left in the circle look away from the cameras, bracing for what comes next. Seconds later gallons of dark green, sticky slime rain down over them. The red circle is now hidden under the sticky goop, but no amount of slime can hide the humiliation on the three contestants' faces. I wish I could say I feel safe on the winner's block, but if I'm not careful in the finals, I could end up in the circle getting sludged and shamed in front of the entire country. I smile for the cameras, but in the background, I can still hear the audience chanting, "Lo-sers, Lo-sers, Lo-sers."

CHAPTER

2

That night, I fly home to Portland. I spend the next few days resting up for what is about to be the toughest four days of my life. The quarterfinal and semifinal rounds each consisted of four obstacle courses—there was one every Saturday, so I had a week to rest in between each course. But there will be no rest during the finals. The final round begins on Thursday with the first obstacle course, followed by three days with a different, harder course each day. At the end of the fourth day, our scores will be added up to determine who wins the prize money and title of Ultimate Warrior.

I spend Sunday and Monday exercising just enough to stay limber. I don't want to overdo it or my body will be too tired. Tuesday night I am back on a plane to Los Angeles.

A van shuttles me from the airport to the upscale hotel I've been staying in. This has been my home this summer for the past eight weekends, during quarterfinals and semifinals, and it will be my home for the next five days until the competition is over. I arrive in my huge room, brush my teeth, text my parents goodnight, then climb under the luxury sheets and fall asleep.

***

The next morning, I brace myself for a long day of madness. The producers of the show want the audience to get to know the finalists better, so the entire day will be spent doing photo shoots and interviews on the sound stage. The producers call them the *Within the Warrior* segments.

I spend an hour in hair and makeup. I'm used to doing my own hair and makeup for gymnastics competitions, but this is way more involved. All I would do for gymnastics was slick my hair up in a bun and slap on bold eye shadow. But today, I have professionals blowing out my hair and applying all kinds of fancy makeup. It takes Ravi and Paul half the time because they basically just get their faces powdered and hair brushed.

Despite the extra makeup, the photo shoot is a lot of fun. They want each of us to show our individual athletic skills, so they've built a small obstacle course on the sound stage for us to pose in. I choose a foam beam and display my walkover and handsprings. The photographer gets an amazing shot of Ravi, a track star, hurdling over the beam. Paul climbs a bouldering wall one-handed, then hangs from his hold upside down, like a monkey. He has no problem showing off.

But when the cameras cut, Paul's smile fades. "Enjoy the spotlight while it lasts," he says to me and Ravi, sneering. Ravi wants to spit something back, but I shoot him a look that says don't bother.

Next are our interviews. Ravi and I listen as Paul pretends to be sweet and innocent. "Why do you think you have what it takes to be the Ultimate Warrior, Paul?" the interviewer asks.

Paul smiles shyly, bowing his head and raising his eyes. *He looks like a puppy*, I think in disgust. "When I began this journey, I didn't know if I had what it takes," Paul responds. "There were so many amazing athletes from all over the country competing. I was overwhelmed. But then I surprised myself by winning regionals and making it past each round."

The interviewer smiles at Paul. "Your humility is so refreshing. Most athletes of your caliber have none."

"I used to be like that, before the accident."

"Of course. You were in a car accident two years ago."

"Two broken legs, a damaged spinal cord. The doctors didn't know if I would live, let alone climb again."

"And yet, here you are."

"Here I am. And I'm just so grateful to be here, I don't take anything for granted anymore."

"Would you be grateful even if you lost?"

Paul pauses. Inside the real Paul must be thinking, *Of course not. I want to destroy everyone and prove I'm the best.* But loveable, on-camera Paul can't say that. I lean in more. I can't wait to hear what he's going to say.

"Every step I take is an achievement, and, I hope, an inspiration to those watching. But I do want to win. I think winning would show the world that, no matter how low you start, you can achieve anything."

"Thank you, Paul. That was very moving. Best of luck in the zone."

"Thank you so much for listening."

The camera cuts and the interviewer wipes a tear away from her eye. "Are you serious?" I groan under my breath.

"The guy is good—real good," Ravi whispers. "That'll be a tough act to follow."

"Why do you sound so impressed by him?"

"Because he knows how to play the game."

"The game is an obstacle course."

"Don't be naive, Fiona. Look around. Cameras. All this." He points to my shining, over-styled hair. "It's not just about the course. It's also about how we look and sound—what people think about us matters."

"Sure, a little, but—"

"Not a little." He sighs and turns away. "It's *crucial* to be likeable, and Paul is a master."

"Sure, but that doesn't mean you have to lie. Paul is hiding who he is. You're a likeable guy because you're honest and nice to others. If people don't like you for who you are, then they're the losers, not you."

Ravi nods. "You're right. You're totally right."

We bump fists, then a set hand leads Ravi to the interview chair. On the way, they pass Paul, who ignores Ravi like he's invisible and leaves the set.

Ravi does great. He's charming, relaxed, and able to make the interviewer laugh at all his jokes. He speaks about his parents. How they came to America from India as poor students and have worked very hard to provide for him and his younger sister. How, even though they work long hours, they attend every event he participates in—track meets, math competitions, choir concerts—to support him. Ravi tells the interviewer he wants to win *Warrior Zone* to make his parents proud and to show them that all their work and support has made a difference in his life. The interviewer may have wiped a tear away for Paul, but after Ravi she needs a box of tissues.

Ravi wishes me luck as I take his place in the chair. Making sure the audience likes me is important, Ravi's right about that. Having thousands of people at home and in the audience root for you is a great mental boost. I want to do everything I can to win them over, starting by delivering a genuine segment.

"Thanks for sitting down with me, Fiona," the interviewer begins.

"Thank you for having me," I say, a little too loudly. I take a deep breath and try to relax.

"You placed first in the semifinals. Were you expecting that?"

"Not at all. After we run the course, we have no idea what our scores are. We're not allowed to watch each other since the course is a surprise. I had no idea how I did on my own, let alone compared to everyone else."

"So did you ever think you were going to lose?"

"I try not to think about whether I win or lose. I just focus on doing my best in the zone."

"And your focus truly shows. Watching you figure out the pattern of the horn wall was awesome. Did you know you were the only warrior not to get hit by a horn?"

"Really? To be honest, my adrenaline was so high, I actually thought the horns could skewer me."

The interviewer throws her head back with a laugh. "You know your safety is always the first priority on *Warrior Zone*."

"Of course. I just got a little *too* in the zone."

She laughs again. "You're funny, Fiona. You're also a very accomplished gymnast. What made you want to compete on *Warrior Zone*?"

She's not the first person to ask this question, so answering is easy at this point. "Well, I've always loved gymnastics. I've been a gymnast since age two, competing since

I was five. I am one of the highest ranked gymnasts in the country. I can do more pull ups than the guys on my school's football team. But as much as I love gymnastics, I had to stop earlier this year. The club I was training with my whole life let me down."

"How so?" the interviewer asks, leaning in closer to me.

I brace myself—this still isn't easy for me to talk about. "I learned my coaches were cheating. They were choosing which gymnasts made the competition team based on whose parents paid the most money. Only five from each club can compete at the elite level, so if you don't get to compete, you don't get national exposure, and you don't get considered for the Olympics. This year I didn't make my club team even though I was the best. My mom explained that my coach had demanded money. I missed my shot at the Olympics because my parents wouldn't cheat."

I pause, taking a deep breath. "That's when I knew I had to try out for *Warrior Zone*. I knew from watching the show for years that it would be my chance to compete on an even playing field. I wanted the chance to win, but more importantly, to win fairly. So whatever happens, I'll know it's a reflection of my performance, nothing else."

The interviewer stares at me, eyebrows raised all the way up. "Wow, Fiona, that is really unfair. Lucky for you, on *Warrior Zone* everyone gets the chance to do their best. What matters more to you, winning or having a chance to do your best?"

"Honestly, just being on *Warrior Zone* gives me peace of mind, win or lose. I can't stand cheaters."

"Spoken like a true athlete. Thank you, Fiona. And good luck in the zone."

We shake hands and I hop out of the chair. I join Ravi, who was watching from the side. "Let's eat, I'm starving."

Ravi nods, without saying anything. "What's up?" I ask. "How'd I do?"

"Good, but—" Ravi pauses.

"Uh-oh. But what?"

"Why did you say you were okay losing?"

"That's not what I said," I respond, confused.

"Well, that's how it sounded."

"I just meant I'm not a sore loser. But being a finalist is pretty cool. I'm obviously going to try to win and, no offense, but I'm in first place. I have a good shot."

"Yeah except now you've given the producers exactly what they need."

"Which is what, exactly?"

"A good loser."

CHAPTER
3

Ravi doesn't go further into his theory, and I don't push to learn more. We eat lunch in the large, room-sized catering tent where we and the rest of the production crew eat all our meals, joking around like everything is normal, and then we finish the rest of our segments. I wedge in a workout before dinner to clear my mind and hopefully tire me out enough so I can sleep through the night.

But despite how much I try to shake it, I can't stop worrying that somehow Ravi was right. *What if the producers did have a say in who won and who lost? If so, even though*

I've done so well, would they pick me to be the loser?

I know some reality television can be pretty fake, but those are the shows where people with big personalities get paid to act out outrageous situations. On *Warrior Zone*, the drama comes from how the warriors perform. We aren't acting. It's exciting because no one knows what will happen ahead of time. It's why people love watching sports. It would be a waste to rig *Warrior Zone* . . . wouldn't it?

I am not a loser, I am not a loser, I repeat to myself over and over as I fall asleep.

***

When I wake up the next morning, the mantra is stuck in my head. Today is the first day of the finals. I need to focus. I need to believe in myself. I need to believe that I am not a loser.

By ten o'clock, I am back on the sound stage, or "in the zone" as we say on the show. I'm getting ready in the start zone, pulling on my helmet and safety harness. Ravi and Paul are nearby, doing the same.

The start zone is a plain hallway that ends at a pair of swinging doors. On the other side of the doors is the obstacle course. Each course's theme is inspired by a different type of ancient warrior. I have no idea what kind of warrior theme I am about to face because we aren't allowed to see the course before we run it. It's always a surprise, which forces us to figure out how to pass each obstacle in the moment. All I know is that today's course will be harder than the Viking course—each one is harder than the one before.

Because I came in first place on the last round, I'll go last. Even though I had the highest score in semifinals, our points reset at the beginning of the finals. So right now, Ravi, Paul, and I are tied with zero points—anyone could win.

Each course is made up of three obstacles. The contestant that makes it the farthest through the course, in the fastest time, gets first place in the round and receives three hundred points. Second place receives two hundred. Third place receives one hundred. I hope to come in first this round, but if for some reason I don't, it's okay. I will have three more courses to run before they add up our points and decide who becomes the Ultimate Warrior.

Paul is up first. A horn signals him to begin and he pushes through the swinging doors. Ravi and I wait in silence. I do a few push-ups, and Ravi stretches his hamstrings. We're expecting to wait a few minutes, but after only seconds we hear another signal chime.

"Your turn, Ravi," a set hand calls out. Ravi and I look at each other, confused for the same reason. That was really quick. Too quick. Either Paul finished insanely fast or he didn't make it far at all.

I slap Ravi on the back, wishing him luck. The start horn blasts and Ravi pushes through the doors.

I jump around to shake out my nerves and get my blood flowing. Then, I still myself and start to count my breaths. One . . . two . . . three—

That's as far as I get before the set hand interrupts me. "Fiona, you're up."

"Already? It's only been one minute," I say to him, alarmed.

"I know," he says with a shrug. "Good luck."

My breathing picks up. My heart pounds. To say I'm nervous would be wrong. I'm terrified. But when the horn blasts, my mind quiets and I take off, through the doors, into complete darkness.

I can hear the crowd off to the side cheering my name. I can hear the announcer mumbling, but can't make out what he's saying. Is he whispering? I can hear my footsteps on the rubber floor. But I can't see anything.

I stop walking. *What if I accidentally step off the course and disqualify myself? Is that why Paul and Ravi finished so quickly?* I kneel down and begin feeling the ground in all directions. I run my hands forward about a foot and suddenly my fingers touch air. The ground comes to an end. If I'd taken one more step, I'd have fallen off that edge into whatever lies below.

Now that I know which way *not* to go, I start searching for the way I *should* go. I feel up and behind me. There's nothing except the doors I came through. I feel my way back to the ground's edge and reach a little bit beyond, first with my arm, then with my leg, sticking it out over the edge. Maybe, just maybe . . . *Yes! There's a wall!* But it's two feet on the other side of the gap. There must be some way to get over there.

I use my leg to scan side to side along the wall. It's pretty wide. Suddenly, my foot runs into something sticking out from the wall. It's long enough for me to touch it with my hands. Instantly I can tell what it is. A sword hilt. I pull on the hilt and sure enough something long and heavy slides out. I can't see it, but I can definitely feel the sword in my hand. *What the heck do I do now?* As if it heard me, a dim, green light shines from the top of the wall. The light blinks like a beacon, calling me up toward it. *But how? With this sword?*

As my eyes adjust, I can see another sword hilt on my right. My heart sinks—I realize what I have to do. I take a few steps back then take a huge leap to the second sword. I grab it tight with my right hand. My legs dangle, with nothing on the slick wall to hold onto. I bring the first sword up and stab it hard into the wall above me. It sinks into to what feels like thick foam, giving me a secure hold. I put my weight on the left sword and repeat the same thing with the right sword. Pulling it out of the wall and stabbing it into the wall above me. I pull up and do this again. Stab, pull up, stab, pull up, climbing my way to the top. I'm six feet from the blinking light. I can finally see the top of the wall. But my palms are sweating, my arms are shaking, and my muscles are screaming in protest. I fight to pull up on the sword, but my body gives out. My hands let go and I fall.

Before I can scream, I land on a soft bed of nets. *I did terribly*, I think. I didn't even make it over the first obstacle. All I can do is hope Ravi and Paul did worse.

I make my way off the nets and onto my feet. As usual, a swarm of cameras surround me. Someone behind them asks, "Tough fall, Fiona. How do you feel?" I'm saved from answering by a set hand. "Fiona, a producer wants to see you. Follow me, please."

I follow him off the sound stage, into a hallway, and up the stairs. The entire time, I'm wondering why a producer would possibly need to see me. *Have I done something wrong?* We come into a booth filled with video equipment. Men and women scroll through yesterday's interview footage of me, Ravi, and Paul. This must be where they edit the show for broadcast.

"Well done against the Ninja, Fiona." A woman in jeans and a T-shirt appears beside me with a bottle of water. Her name is Sarah and she is one of the producers of *Warrior Zone*. She and her coworkers run every part of the show. They design all the courses and create all the scoring and timing rules. They even came up with yesterday's interview questions. Even though this is a reality show, the producers make most of it up. Everything except who wins, of course.

"Ninja? Is that what that was? I couldn't really tell," I say, eyeing the water.

"Please, take it. Hydrate." Sarah hands me the bottle. I've met Sarah once before, when

Ravi and I showed up for quarterfinals, lost and nervous. She showed us where to sign in and wished us luck. I remember thinking she seemed cool, but I haven't seen her since. *Why does she want to see me now?*

"Thank you," I say before swallowing half the bottle.

"You placed first again, by the way."

I nearly spit the water out. "What?" I splutter. "I didn't even make it to the top of the first obstacle!"

"No one did. But you made it the farthest."

"But Paul is a climber. I thought for sure he scaled that wall faster than I could."

"I'm sure he would have if he managed to find the wall before falling off the edge. Same with Ravi. You were the only one to figure it out."

I shake my head, baffled. I was not expecting this at all.

"There won't be a ceremony until scores from all four of the finals courses are calculated," Sarah continues. "Anything could happen on the next three."

"Of course."

She looks at me, her smile faltering. "Have a seat, please." The editors leave the room and Sarah and I take their seats. "As you know, ratings are extremely important to any television show. The more viewers we have, the more popular and beloved our show, the longer we can stay on the air. As producers, we have to make sure the viewers get something they'll never forget. I'd like to tell you about our plan for this year."

"Your plan?" I ask, growing uneasy. "Isn't the plan to see who wins and then award them?"

Sarah cocks her head to the side and frowns. "I wish it were that simple. See, odds are that you are going to win the next three courses and leave the boys in the dust. The problem with that is we can't have four episodes where the same thing happens. Why will people want to watch something so predictable? They won't. They'll turn off their televisions, and we will have a problem." Sarah smiles at me sweetly, as if she's just explained something simple.

I shake my head, trying to understand. "So you're saying you have a problem because you think I might do well?"

"Of course not, Fiona. We think you're amazing. But here's the thing. It would be a better story, give us better ratings, if Paul were to be the Ultimate Warrior. If you win, no one will be surprised. But everyone will be surprised if Paul, the underdog, currently in last place, comes from behind for the win. And, as you know, Paul has been recovering from serious injuries. Seeing his rehabilitation take him to the top will warm everyone's hearts. They'll remember this season for years to come."

I stare at Sarah, horrified. "Is this a joke?"

Sarah sighs, then her face brightens. "You will of course be paid."

"For what?"

"For losing."

"You mean *if* I lose?" I ask, still a bit unsure where she's going with this.

Sarah's face droops back into a frown. She sighs again. "I know this is hard, but you have to understand what I'm saying. We need you to pretend to lose. To fall, slow down, struggle—whatever it takes. We will coach you through where and how to do this to create maximum drama. In exchange you will be paid ten thousand dollars for each course you lose and twenty thousand for the final course. You will make even more than you would have as the winner."

"But that's cheating," I spit, jumping to my feet. My face is hot with anger. "I came on this show because I wanted a fair shot. Now you're telling me the game is rigged?"

Sarah stands and lays a calming hand on my shoulder. "Fiona, the game isn't rigged. This is all part of the game, a very fair game. It's just that you're only now learning the rules."

I can feel tears forming in my eyes against my will. Sarah sees them. "I'm really sorry, Fiona." She pulls me in for a hug. "You're still going to have fun. You're still going to be a winner, just in a different way. I promise."

CHAPTER
4

I walk to lunch feeling numb. My body is shivering from my anger. I can't believe this is happening. After everything I've been through, I've wound up with cheaters—again. I came to *Warrior Zone* to get away from this, for a chance at something authentic and fair. Instead I learn it's all a lie.

I've watched teenagers compete on *Warrior Zone* for years, and for years I envied them, yearned for a chance to be like them. Warriors. Champions. *But were they really warriors or were they cheaters too?*

I wander into the catering tent. I'm not

hungry, but I need to find Ravi. I need to talk about this with him, to see if he thinks it's as insane as I do, to ask him if he knew already and if that's why he was so cryptic yesterday. But mostly I just need a friend to calm me down.

There's no sign of Ravi at lunch, so I grab an apple and take the shuttle to my hotel. I call my parents to check in and let them know how things are going. The episodes haven't aired yet, so I'm not allowed to tell them any results. I'm not sure if I'm allowed to tell them what Sarah told me, but I don't have the heart to anyway. My parents pulled me out of my gymnastics club as soon as they learned my coach was cheating. I can't tell them their daughter is about to become a cheater too.

I stay in my room the rest of the night worrying over what to do. The producers run the show. I have to do what they say. *But could I live with myself if I do?*

I fall asleep without an answer.

***

A good athlete knows there's nothing more important than a good night's sleep. When I wake up, my mind has cleared and I know what I must do. I am not a loser and I am definitely not a cheater. I'm not here for money, either. I came here to do my best, to show the country what I can do, and I'm not going to let anyone stop me.

I'm getting ready to head to the sound stage when my phone rings. "Hello?" I answer.

"Fiona? It's Sarah. How are you feeling?"

"I feel great," I say with fake enthusiasm.

"Oh," she says, surprised at my change of tone. "That's great. Well, I'm calling to go over today's routine."

"Routine? Is that what you call pretending to lose?"

Sarah takes a deep breath. "Yes. I know, it seems silly."

"It's cheating," I correct her. I don't want to make this easy for her. "So what's the routine?"

"Today's course is inspired by ancient Gladiators of the Roman Colosseum. First, you'll face a dungeon full of chains that you'll need to cross without falling. Second, there's the sand pit on the Colosseum floor, which you'll also need to make it through. The third obstacle is a spear trapeze, where you'll swing from one spear-shaped trapeze up to the next. This is where we'd like you to fall."

"Fall? Off a trapeze? Did you forget that I'm an award-winning gymnast? I would never fall off a trapeze."

"Right, well, that's why it's exciting, isn't it? No one will expect it. Also, because you'll have a lot of control, you'll know how to make your fall look real. Sound easy enough?"

I pause, forcing myself not to say anything rude. Instead I say, in my perkiest voice, "Sounds great! Wish me luck!"

An hour later, I'm waiting in the start zone for my turn. Ravi waves hello but stays in his corner, stretching alone. We haven't spoken since this time yesterday. *Is he avoiding me?* I wonder. But now is not the time to talk. We both need to focus and prepare—we have a course to run.

To my surprise, it's Paul who wants to talk.

He crosses the room to stand next to me. "I just wanted to say good luck. You're doing so well out there," he says, loud enough for people around us to hear. Then he lowers his voice and whispers, "And you're going to need all the luck you can get because my mistakes are in the past. I'm coming for you." He glares at me with threatening eyes, but they quickly brighten into a smile and he walks away. *What a jerk.* I almost want to thank him. He's just given me one more reason to do what I'm going to do.

Ravi is up first since he came in last place against the Ninja. He disappears through the door and it's just me and Paul for five minutes. Paul goes next. I watch the clock and he is gone for about the same time as Ravi. It's hard to know without watching if he got farther or not.

Finally, it's my turn. The start horn blasts and I sprint through the doors. Like Sarah said, the first course is a web of chains hanging from a low ceiling in a room that looks like a dungeon. I grab a chain and swing through, taking the time I need to avoid any mistakes while still pushing myself as fast as I can go.

The more slowly I move, the more energy I'll waste. Better to zoom through.

I make it through the dungeon of chains into the next obstacle. The sand pit is a large pool of sand surrounded by walls painted to look like the Colosseum. I trudge through the sand pit, careful to avoid areas where the sand appears to be sinking. *Quicksand*, I think, as I spot a patch ahead of me and change direction.

I make it through the sand pit and up a few stairs to the first of five trapeze bars. Each one is higher than the next, so I have to swing both forward and upward. This would be a challenge for someone who has never done the uneven bars. Luckily, I've been doing them for years. If I were going to do what Sarah wanted, it would be easy for me to fake a fall. I'd mistime my swing and shorten my jump. Maybe I'd even let my fingertips graze the bar as I fell to make it look like I came close.

But I have no intention of doing what Sarah wants—I am *not* a cheater.

I grab the first bar and swing myself up to a standing position. From here, I jump to the second, the third, the fourth, and then to the final bar. Instead of standing on the bar, I decide to show off. I swing over the bar into a handstand once, twice, then a third time, before I flip off and stick a perfect landing in the finish zone. I hear the audience explode with applause, so I blow a kiss their way. *If the producers want a performance, they'll get one*, I think triumphantly.

I make my way off the course with the crowd chanting my name: "Fio-NA! Fio-NA!" I run over to them and bow, blowing more kisses. They love it. Even the announcer is cheering for me: "Let's give it up for Fiona! Another amazing round. Our girl is unbeatable!"

Unbeatable is right.

I make my way off stage toward Ravi, who is staring at me, astonished. Beside him, Paul glares at me, furious and speechless. This is not how he thought today was going to go. But before I can reach them, Sarah comes up to me, smiling, and whispers in my ear. "Come with me—now." I follow her off the stage and into a hallway. Her smile disappears immediately. "You did not do what we discussed."

"No, I didn't cheat. But you said you wanted ratings, right? Listen to that crowd. They love that I am unbeatable. Let me keep going. Give me the chance of a fair game, and I'll give you the best story for your show. And if I take a fall, or someone else beats me, then there's your surprise twist. Either way, you win."

Sarah's face darkens, past disappointment, past anger, to something more alarming. When she speaks, her voice is almost a whisper. "Wake up, Fiona. It doesn't work like that. You don't decide how things go, okay? We do. Everyone you've beaten so far, we paid to lose to you. The only reason you've made it this far is because we wanted you to make it."

This hits me hard. So it's true—the game's been rigged all along. It probably has been for years. But the cheating stops with me. "You can't make me cheat. And you can't kick me off. The crowd loves me too much."

Sarah's jaw tightens. "This is your final warning. You have no idea what we can do to make sure you play along. I don't suggest you find out."

Sarah blows past me and heads down the hallway. When she's gone, I let out a breath I've been holding in. In this moment, I realize that I'm not competing against Paul and Ravi. The true warriors I'm battling are the producers themselves.

CHAPTER
5

I really need some air.

I find it at the hotel, which has a large rooftop pool. The sun is out and it's hot, but there's only one person up here. Ravi is sitting on the edge of the pool with his legs in the water. I sit beside him and start taking off my shoes. "Ravi, you're a genius."

"What's up, Fi?"

"Eh, you know. Trying to accept the fact that this *reality* show is faker than Santa Claus."

He laughs as I dip my feet into the warm water. "Yeah, I know what you mean."

"So Sarah talked to you about cheating? When?"

"Before we filmed our *Within the Warrior* interviews. That's why I was trying to warn you. When did you find out? Just now?"

"Nope," I say, shaking my head. "Yesterday."

"But you—"

"Didn't do what they wanted? No way! Why did you?"

Ravi hangs his head low so his face hovers over the water. I can see his reflection looking back at him. "At first, I was angry. Very angry. But when they explained I'd be guaranteed more money than if I actually won, I couldn't say no."

I kick the water hard. I can't believe what I'm hearing. "You did it for the money? I thought you were better than that, man."

Ravi pulls his feet out of the water and hugs his knees to his chest. "You don't understand, Fiona. My parents work hard to give me every opportunity they can, and it's expensive. They don't even know I know, but I hear them at night, after they think I've gone to bed, talking about their money situation. They're barely getting by. But if I lose, I get forty thousand dollars. That money could really help them, and I owe it to them to help when I can. I'm sorry if you thought I was someone better. I guess I just can't afford to be." Ravi buries his head in his knees, making himself into a ball.

I feel like such a jerk. I want to curl into a ball too and throw myself into this pool and sink to the bottom where no one can find me. Instead, I scoot closer to Ravi and put my arm around him. "I'm sorry I said that. I didn't know. Will you forgive me?"

Slowly, Ravi nods. He reaches his arm out and pats my back without raising his head off his knees. "I don't want to cheat, Fi. I want to make my parents proud. If I lose, even if I explain that the producers made me do it and that I did it to help them, they won't be proud. I don't know how to help them and make them proud at the same time. It's impossible."

"Me too. I mean, my parents took me out of my gymnastics club when they found out it was corrupt. I can only imagine what they'd think if they knew how crooked things were here."

I lie down against the warm concrete and stare up at the empty blue sky. *There must be a way to win fairly, and to get Ravi the money he needs.*

I bolt upright. "I've got it! I know how we can do this!"

Ravi lifts his head and squints at me. "How?"

"It's so simple," I laugh. "They can't kick both of us off, right? They can't have a fake competition if there's no one to compete. So if we both agree to boycott their rules and play fairly, they can't stop us."

Ravi scratches his hair. "Yeah, that could work. I mean, we still have to beat Paul, but that's doable."

"If we do our best, one of us will probably come in first place. If somehow Paul magically beats us, we'll still get the money from losing."

"So we try to win, but we get paid either way," says Ravi, a slow smile spreading across his face.

"Exactly! And whatever money I get, you can have."

"What?" Ravi looks shocked.

"I mean it," I reassure him. "I was never in this for the money. My parents don't need it as much as yours. And you're my friend. We help each other. If the money will help you, then I want you to have it. End of story." I stick out my hand for him to shake. "It's the perfect plan, admit it."

"Yeah. It is," Ravi admits.

"So are you in?"

Ravi nods. "Yeah. I'm in." We shake on it, then he grins mischievously. "Sorry, Fi."

"For what?"

"For this!" Ravi jumps and yanks me with him, face first into the pool.

CHAPTER 6

It's Saturday morning and Ravi, Paul, and I are back in the start zone, warming up for the third challenge. An hour ago, Sarah called my hotel room before I left to tell me my routine for today's course. "You're going to struggle climbing the first obstacle and then you're going to fall before the beginning of the second . . . if you make it that far," she had instructed.

"What do you mean *if*?" I asked. Her cheerful tone made me uneasy.

"You'll see." She hung up without any further explanation.

Ravi and I compare instructions as we warm up in the waiting room. Sarah called him as well. She told him the same thing—to struggle in the first climb and fall before the beginning of the second obstacle. She also hinted he may not make it that far. "There's never a guarantee we will make it through any course. And we know this one is going to be tough. She's just trying to get in our heads," I assure him. "She's probably taking extra care to make sure you play along since I've turned out to be a giant pain."

"Do you think she suspects anything?" Ravi asks, lowering his voice.

I fold my arm over my chest, stretching my bicep. "It doesn't matter. She can't do anything about it."

But can she? I remember her warning after yesterday's course. "You have no idea what we can do to make sure you play along," she'd said. I try to put it out of my head.

I can tell Ravi is nervous. Not about our plan, but for the same reason I am: this is the second to last round before they determine the winner. I'm in first place with six hundred and sixty points. Ravi is in second place with three hundred and forty points. Paul is in third with three hundred and twenty points. Since we're so close to the end of the competition, finishing as many obstacles as we can is even more important because doing so will earn us more points. We get thirty points for every obstacle we cross.

Like the other rounds, this course will be harder than the one before. Unlike the other rounds, this is the first course that we're allowed to see ahead of time. We also get to watch each other's turn. The idea is that the course is so physically challenging that knowing ahead of time won't give us an advantage.

A few moments later, we walk through the doors and catch our first glimpse of what we're facing. I can tell right away what kind of warrior inspired this round. Today we will face the Knight.

I stare at the course in awe. Paul pushes past Ravi and me to get a closer look. But I can see it just fine from here. It's massive. And it looks incredibly difficult.

The course starts with a series of vertical, shiny nets, each one hung above the other. The highest one looks about eighty feet in the air. From here, the nets look like they are made from a knight's chainmail. Instead of the wide squares usually found on climbing nets, the holes are only large enough for one finger at a time. Our shoes won't fit at all, which means this climb completely relies on upper body strength. The net is also made of metal instead of rope. And metal is harder to grasp. Sarah instructed me and Ravi to struggle here, but she didn't need to. It will be a struggle no matter what. We'll have to climb all eighty feet of the chainmail and slide down a metal slide to part two.

The second obstacle is a moat-shaped pool of water with stones floating on its surface. The task is to cross the moat by hopping from stone to stone. However, we have to do this dressed in heavy armor that weighs about fifty pounds. This is where Sarah wants me and Ravi to fall, which we can only do if we've survived the chainmail climb.

Finally, if we are lucky enough to cross the moat, we have to complete the last obstacle. A sword is wedged into a boulder and we have to pull it out. It's just like the myth where young King Arthur pulled the sword from the stone—except *our* stone is on a narrow, spinning pedestal. We will have to jump onto it, manage not to fall off, then somehow pull the sword from the stone, and jump down into the finish zone.

I'm exhausted just looking at it. Ravi looks like he might puke. Paul is pacing and biting his nails. In the distance, I can hear the announcer speaking to the crowd. "I don't know how our warriors are going to make it through this one, folks. I just don't know."

A signal chimes, calling us to line up in the start zone. Paul, still in last place, will go first. I can tell he's anxious. I'm not sure why, but even though he's been rude and unfriendly, I suddenly feel bad for him. "Good luck," I tell him, as Ravi and I head to our waiting positions. Paul looks up and shoots me a cold glare. The start horn blasts and Paul's turn begins.

Paul sprints toward the chainmail climb. He makes it up with the lightning speed of an experienced climber. I have no hope of beating him there. After just a minute and a half, he is down the slide.

The audience gasps as Paul, wearing the heavy armor, jumps from stone to stone across the moat. He teeters a few times but never falls into the murky water.

On the other side of the moat, Paul sheds the armor and jumps for the spinning platform. He lands with his arms on the platform and his feet dangling beneath him. He tries to swing his legs up onto the platform, but he can't get a firm hold. He's spinning fast—he must be getting dizzy. I can see his arms slipping. He fights to keep his grasp, but finger by finger his strength gives out and he falls onto a safety net below.

"Oooooh," winces the audience, but a second later they're applauding. That was an impressive run for anyone, let alone Paul. He hasn't made it to the last obstacle since semifinals.

I give Ravi a pat on the back. "Don't worry. You can beat that."

"Yeah, yeah," he says, nodding.

"Make sure you jump for the sword, not the platform!" I shout after him. "It's easier to hold on to. He tried to hold the platform, but it's too narrow. That's why he fell."

Ravi looks back at me, expressionless. No smile. No thumbs-up. Just a blank stare. *He's just in the zone. Right?*

The horn blasts and Ravi is off. He starts up the chainmail climb. He's not going as quickly or effortlessly as Paul, but I'd be surprised if he was. He's doing well though, slowly pulling his weight up each length of metal net. Ravi eventually makes it to the top and zooms down the slide.

He advances to the moat. Once he has on all the armor, he hops to the first stone. Then, disaster strikes. He lands with his feet only halfway on the stone. His limbs flail,

trying to find balance. But they never do.
Ravi falls with a hard splash into the dark water
of the moat.

He fell at the beginning of the second
obstacle. Exactly where Sarah told him to fall.

I try to push dark thoughts from my mind.
*Ravi is my friend and we had an agreement. If
he fell, it was while trying his best. He wouldn't
cheat. Would he?*

Ravi emerges from the moat, covered head
to toe in thick, muddy water. He makes his
way off the course and the set hands walk him,
wrapped in a towel, back toward the waiting
room. As he passes me, he keeps his eyes
glued to the ground. He doesn't look up at me.
Doesn't wish me good luck.

"Ravi?" I say as he passes. But he doesn't
stop, and he doesn't say anything. It's as good
as a confession.

The horn blasts for me to start and I run
toward the first obstacle. *Ravi cheated. Ravi,
my friend, betrayed me.* I try to focus as I climb,
but I can't get these thoughts out of my head.
Ravi cheated. I'm in this alone. Distracted, I lose

my hold on the net. I fall to the end of one net
before I jam my fingers into the holes. I stop
so fast my finger bones nearly break. That was
close. And painful. I pause for a moment. I let
the anger of Ravi's betrayal build up. I feel it
burning, the pressure of it behind my eyes. I
feel it turn to water and begin to trickle out of
my eyes. *Oh no, I can't be crying. The audience is
watching. People will see this on TV. I have to get
ahold of myself.*

I push my tears back and force myself
upward. I'm not sure how, but I make it to the
top. I'm too afraid to think or feel anything,
so I slide down and try to get focused. I pull
on the armor and jump to the first stone.
I wobble, landing dangerously off balance.
Muscle memory built up over years of balance
beam work switches on and my body steadies
itself. *I can do this.*

I take a deep breath and look to the next
stone. I calculate the jump, get my footing, and
leap. I land safely in the middle of the second
stone. I look to the third stone, an even shorter
jump than the last. I measure the jump, bend

my knees, and take my leap. I land with both feet on the stone, but an instant later they slip out from under me. My shoulder crashes on the stone before I slip sideways, landing in the murky water with a loud *splat*.

CHAPTER

7

The heavy armor pushes me deep into the muddy moat. As I sink, the gunk seeps into my hair, my clothes, and under my socks. A set hand runs over and helps me out of the moat, then out of the armor. Even though the armor was covering me, I am dripping with mud. The set hand holds out a towel. "No thanks," I say. "I need more than a towel."

A few cameras swirl up to me, making sure to record evidence of my surprise failure. I try to wipe a patch of hair off my cheek but end up smearing mud on my face, making it worse.

The cameras leave and I finally have an exit path. All I want now is to get out of these clothes and into a shower before this gets any worse. But before I can take a step, Sarah appears with a big, smug grin on her face. "Come with me," she says.

"Like this?"

"Just like that." I can tell she's enjoying my humiliation. She leads the way, and I follow reluctantly.

Sarah walks me past the buzzing audience. The announcer sighs, "Poor Fiona," into the microphone as I pass. We leave the sound stage, walk down a hallway, and get into an elevator. Sarah pushes the top button. I search her expression for a hint of where we're going, but she just gazes back at me with the same smug grin on her face. *Maybe they're finally kicking me off*, I worry. *Did I score so badly that the audience won't miss me anymore?*

"How did I do?" I ask, not sure I even want to hear the answer.

Sarah's grin widens. "Pretty bad. You came in last. So much for unbeatable."

I wish I hadn't asked.

The elevator arrives on the top level and the doors open to a floor of sparkling marble. I step out after Sarah and it's like we've entered another planet. Televisions line the walls. Facing each one is a thick, soft couch. I would do anything to flop onto one of those right now. But Sarah leads me past them, and we come to an office at the end of the hallway. "After you," she says, waving me inside.

I walk through the door into a massive conference room. The wall on one side is made of floor-to-ceiling windows that look out over the entire city of Los Angeles. The wall opposite it is filled with four screens, all displaying a different reality show. In the middle of the room is a large conference table. Seated at the table are a dozen men and women in very polished business suits.

"Welcome, Fiona," says one of the suits. He's shorter and older than the others, and he's sitting at the head of the table. He's also completely bald.

"What's up?" I respond, making my voice

sound as casual as I can. I'm nervous, but I
don't want them to see it.

Sarah closes the door behind her and
takes a seat at the table with the suits. I can
tell they're trying to intimidate me—they've
got me outnumbered and alone in a place I've
never been. I'm suddenly grateful to be covered
in mud. I shake off my arms, sending droplets
into the plush white carpet. Their faces flinch
in unison, as if the mud hit them directly.
"Oops, sorry about that," I say, pretending to
look innocent. I'm so *not* sorry.

"You're so good at making a mess, aren't
you Fiona?" the bald guy snaps.

"I'm good at a lot of things . . . Sorry, I
didn't catch your name."

"My name is Diego. I am the head producer
of *Warrior Zone*, which means I'm everyone's
boss. Including yours."

"I don't work for you," I retort. "I'm
a contestant."

"Right now, you're a nuisance. I'm sorry
being on this show hasn't been what you
thought it would be, but that's your fault,

not ours. This is how our show works—it's
not up to you. You have had two chances
to change your behavior. We're not giving
you another."

"So does that mean I'm fired, *boss*?" I don't
usually talk to anyone like this, but everything
about this guy goes against everything I
stand for. He is the ultimate cheater, the one
who tells the others to make us cheat, the
one who makes everyone here believe what
they're doing is okay when it really isn't. If he
wants to push me around, then I'm going to
push back.

"You're not fired," he says to my surprise.
"You were right about what you said to Sarah.
The audience loves you. If we got rid of you,
our ratings would suffer. But we don't need to
get rid of you to make you do what you're told."

I roll my eyes. "Why don't you just say
what you want to say so I can get out of here?
I could really use a shower before the crud you
put in that moat does permanent damage to my
roots." A few of the suits chuckle. Diego shoots
them a sharp look and their smiles vanish.

"You were supposed to slip on the first stone today. You slipped on the third. Want to know why?"

"Uh, because it was a super hard challenge and no one is perfect, not even me?" I flash him a princess-worthy smile.

He smiles back. "No," he says, mimicking my snarky tone. "You slipped because we made you slip. We assumed you wouldn't obey Sarah, so we made sure you would slip on the third stone instead. We could have made you screw up on the fourth or fifth stone, but we chose the third. And that's where you fell. My point is that we were in control the entire time. We have ways of making sure you do what we want, whether you wish to cooperate or not. We can grease any part of the course we choose. We can wipe away the evidence before the next warrior takes their turn. And we can do this without a single person noticing. We did it today, while everyone watched. If I want you to lose, you will lose."

Suddenly a sense of calm washes over me. All I want is to get back to my room so

I can figure out a plan, so I can wipe that self-satisfied smirk off Diego's face. "Do you enjoy being a filthy cheater, Diego? Or do you convince yourself that what you're doing is fair?" I say, straightening up.

"I don't have to play fair. It's my show, my rules."

"Okay, *boss*. Now what?"

"There is one course left. Paul will win. We will give you instructions on where to fall. If you obey, you will receive your compensation. In fact, we will pretend you obeyed the whole time and pay you the entire forty thousand we promised."

"If you think I'm here for the money, you must not know many true athletes."

"We figured you'd say something like that. So here's the deal. If you don't listen to us and you try to win anyway, we will use our methods and make sure you fall. You won't know how or where on the course we'll do it, but we will make sure you go down. If it comes to this, you will lose—and neither you nor your friend Ravi will receive any compensation."

"What?" I say, tensing.

"Yes, Fiona. If you don't follow our rules, both you and Ravi will be punished. Or you can just play nice and everybody wins."

I glare at them. *These adults in their suits act like they rule the world. But their abuse of power is actually ruining it.*

"You can leave, Fiona. Get that shower before you suffer permanent damage."

I smirk at him, then I bow my head and flip my hair onto my back. Flecks of mud from my hair spray at the table, sprinkling the producers' perfectly tailored suits with black, muddy water. They all flinch and jump back from the table.

"I'll show myself out," I say. I make sure to wipe the mud off my shoes and into the carpet before I walk out the door.

CHAPTER

8

It takes me half an hour to wash all of the sludge away. I'm in pajamas wrapping my hair in a towel when someone knocks on my door. I peek through the peephole. It's Ravi. My stomach turns to ice and the anger I felt on the course flares up again. He lied to me. He betrayed me. And now everything is worse—for both of us. *I should just ignore him,* I think.

Ravi knocks again. "Fiona? I know you're in there. Can we talk?"

My best friend Cici and I met in gymnastics class when we were five. Over the years, we became as close as sisters. The day my parents found out my coach was corrupt, they learned Cici's parents had been paying him side money the whole time.

"Fi, please. Just open the door. I need you to know I'm sorry."

After I found out, I texted Cici a few times, asking how long she had known and why she hadn't told me. I asked if we could just talk, but she never texted back. She never said anything. She was my best friend and then, *poof*, she disappeared from my life.

This last thought makes me open the door. Ravi's been a bad friend, but at least he's still here.

I let him in and we sit on the couch in silence for a few seconds. "I'm really sorry," he finally says. "I panicked when Paul did so well. I was a coward. I betrayed you."

"And you cheated."

"Yes. I was afraid if I didn't cheat I'd still lose, and then I wouldn't have the money or the points. I should have known you had my back. Instead, I chickened out and didn't have

yours. I'm disgusted with myself. I promise
you, I'll never flake like that again."

"What do you mean *again*?"

"I mean let's win this together, no cheating.
There's one more round. We can still do this."

I shake my head. So much has happened
that he doesn't know about yet. He thinks
there's still a chance. I have to break it to him.
"It's not that simple anymore."

"Why not?"

"Because we can't win. I fell today because
the producers made me. They have some way
of making the course slippery wherever and
whenever they want."

"What? That's impossible," Ravi says,
stunned.

"They did it to me today—my feet slipped
from under me. Then Sarah took me upstairs
to meet her boss. He's a jerk, by the way. He
told me they could do this slipperiness thing
wherever they want, and that they can even
wipe everything clean so it doesn't affect the
next contestant. He said he's going to use it to
make sure I lose."

Ravi paces around the room, taking this all in, while I stretch out on the couch, exhausted. Then he freezes in the middle of the room. "They specifically said the word 'wipe'?"

"Yeah, why?"

"Because I saw . . ." He trails off, lost in a thought.

"You saw what?"

"You know the set hands? They all have towels. They handed me one after I fell in that crud. I've also seen them wiping down the course between runs."

"Wait, you don't think . . ."

"There are dozens of set hands all over the place. No one is paying any attention to them. They could easily squirt an oil or gel on the course when the audience and cameras are focused on something else and then literally wipe it off with their towels after the contestant slips."

I sit up so fast, the towel falls off my head. "I bet you're right—it's just the set hands! And I bet, if we pay attention, we can catch them in the act again . . ."

"And then we can just avoid that part of the course!" Ravi practically yells, finishing my thought. We're both starting to get excited, but then I remember something that makes me stop.

Ravi sees my expression change. "What's wrong?"

"It doesn't matter if we know where they slick the course. The producers warned me if I don't fall where I'm told, I don't get any money. And neither do you."

Ravi shrugs this away. "Then forget the losing money. One of us is going to have to come in first. The winner gets a huge check right away, during the awards ceremony. It's part of the show. They have to give it to us no matter what. The entire audience is expecting it. They may not have to pay us for losing, but there's no way they can avoid paying us for winning."

"And if neither of us wins?"

"Then we don't deserve any money. That's playing fair."

"I can't argue with that! So we're doing this?" I ask, barely believing it.

Ravi nods, grinning. "We are. For real this time."

I'm so happy that I start jumping in circles. Only then do I notice him. Leaning in the doorway, listening to our every word, is Paul.

CHAPTER

9

"Cheaters," Paul calls us, spitting out the word.

Ravi grabs Paul by the arm and pulls him inside my room. I shut the door behind them. It must not have closed all the way when I let Ravi in.

"Were you spying on us?" I ask Paul, creeped out.

"We're not cheaters," Ravi says at the same time, his hand still holding Paul's arm.

"Let him go," I tell Ravi.

"I don't want him running to the producers."

"You can't stop me," Paul says, struggling

to free himself from Ravi's hold. Frustrated, he gives up, then says threateningly, "I'm going to tell them you're cheating."

"WE'RE NOT CHEATING!" Ravi and I shout together.

"I heard you talking all the way down the hall!" Paul shouts back. "You said 'We're doing this.' I heard it. You're planning something."

Ravi lets Paul go, but I lock the door and stand in front of it. Paul doesn't understand what he heard, and I'm not letting him go until he does.

"Listen, Paul," I say, "Ravi and I don't want to cheat. The producers want us to. We were planning a way to *avoid* cheating."

Paul looks from me to Ravi in disbelief. He's not buying it.

"We're serious, Paul. They want us to lose on purpose. Didn't they tell you? You're the one they want to win."

I can see that Paul's thinking fast. When he hears this last part, his face darkens. "You're liars. You're just making this up so I don't tell the producers."

I groan in frustration. Ravi thrusts his arms in the air. *How can we get through to him?*

An idea hits me. I step away from the door. "Go ahead, Paul. You're free to go." Both Ravi and Paul stare at me in surprise. "Go tell the producers that Ravi and I are going to cheat. I promise you nothing would make them happier. And if we're lying, then we'll get in trouble anyway. You can't lose."

Paul glares coldly at me like he did this morning. "Is this another mind trick?" he asks. "Like earlier when you wished me luck to throw me off my game?"

Now it's my turn to be surprised. No wonder he gave me that look. He thought I was trying to hurt him. "That wasn't a trick, Paul. I meant it."

"Yeah right," he says, shaking head. "I know what you two think of me. You hate me."

"That's because you're a jerk to us," Ravi responds.

I shoot Ravi a look. "Not helping."

"Yeah, well, I'm not here to make friends," says Paul. "I'm here to win. For my brother."

"Your brother?" Ravi asks.

"He's the reason I got into climbing to begin with. He's the reason I still do it today. He died. In the car accident."

Ravi looks at me with wide eyes, not sure what to do. Paul stares at the ground, not moving. "I'm so sorry, Paul. We never knew . . . You didn't say anything about him in your interview. That's . . . awful." I reach out and lay a hand on Paul's shoulder. It rests there for a second, then he pulls away.

"And he's the reason I'm not going to let two cheaters keep me from winning," Paul spits out in disgust.

Before Ravi and I can say another word, Paul opens the door and slams it shut behind him as he leaves. Ravi bangs his head against the wall. "He's probably going straight to the producers to sell us out," he says.

"Maybe. I guess we'll know tomorrow."

"This is probably the only game in the world where we get in trouble for *not* cheating," Ravi says. That makes me laugh so hard I have to lie down.

After Ravi leaves, I try to sleep. I don't manage to get much rest.

The next morning, I try to eat but I'm too nervous. Because Paul may rat us out. Because this course will be the hardest we've ever faced. Because this course will also be slicked with oil. Because I've made it so close to finally winning something, winning fairly, for the first time in my life.

Someone sits down next to me at breakfast. I'm hoping it's Ravi, but I look up to see Sarah. Only now do I realize she didn't called me earlier with today's cheating routine. My heart pounds fast. If Paul went to her, I'm about to find out.

But Sarah only has four words for me: "Fall from the chains." Then she leaves.

I sigh a long exhale, relieved to know Paul didn't tell on us. *Did he believe us after all?*

Paul, Ravi, and I gather in the start zone. The three of us are silent as we gape up at the monstrous final course standing before us. They're calling it Frankenstein. It's a blend of the hardest obstacles we've faced so far in the finals.

First is the climbing wall we faced in the
Ninja. Today we must climb it blindfolded
instead of in the dark. Next are the chain ropes
from the Gladiator's Colosseum—this is where
Sarah wants me to fall. Then, the Knight's
sword in the stone is mounted on its spinning
platform. And finally, there is a long tunnel at
the end of the course. It's unclear what we will
face inside it, but we must make it through to the
other end and drop down into the finish zone.

Right now, I am in first place with eight
hundred and forty points. Paul is in second
with seven hundred and thirteen. Ravi is in last
place with six hundred and twelve. Because this
is the last and hardest course, every obstacle is
worth forty points. And instead of first place
earning three hundred points, this time it's
worth eight hundred, which means all three of
us still have a chance to win.

Instead of going in order, we flip a coin to
determine who goes first. Paul doesn't make
eye contact with me or Ravi the entire time.
The coin determines that Ravi will go first,
I'll go next, and Paul will go last.

Ravi and I look at each other, a silent signal to start looking for the oil. We study the course, watching the set hands as they roam around. They all look like they're doing their normal job of setting the course and making sure it's safe. Ravi taps me on the shoulder and points to the sword in the stone. A set hand is kneeling on the platform. We both walk a few feet closer for a better look. The set hand stands up and hops down. A few moments later she hits a button under the platform and it begins to spin. We follow her as she walks away from the course, and then we see it—she tucks a bottle into her pocket. The bottle looked small, but it definitely looked like something you could use to squirt oil from. *She just oiled the spinning platform!*

"How am I supposed to get around that?" Ravi asks. "She probably slicked the entire platform. I'll fall right off."

"You'll be fine," I assure him. "Jump to grab the sword. Your feet will slip but you can hold on to the sword until you get your balance."

Ravi nods but looks uncertain. "I'll do my best."

"You got this, Ravi!"

Ravi lines up at the starting line. A set hand ties on his blindfold. Seconds later, the start horn blasts and he takes off cautiously toward the Ninja task. Ravi feels his way down the ramp. This time he knows what to expect and can reach over the gap between the ramp and the wall. He finds the swords in the wall and uses them to make the climb with ease.

At the top, he throws off his blindfold and makes it into the dungeon of chains. Like me, Ravi was instructed to fall here. But he doesn't. He carefully swings from one chain to the next. He crosses through the dungeon to a stationary platform. Here he studies the spinning platform with the sword in the stone, ten feet away from him. He has to make the jump, not just to the platform but to the sword itself. It's his only way to get a sure grip. Ravi watches it spin around once, twice, again, again, then finally he makes a running leap and . . . catches the sword! He clutches it tight, his feet slipping on the oiled platform. After a few tries, Ravi manages to stand on his tiptoes and balance on the platform. Slowly, without moving any part of his body except his hands, he pulls the sword out of the stone.

Now he only has one obstacle left. Ravi jumps down from the spinning platform and into the tube. The instant Ravi disappears inside, it's clear what happens in the tube. The tube begins to tip at a dangerous angle, first to the left, then to the right, back and forth like an invisible hand shaking a soda bottle. After what feels like hours, Ravi appears at the other end. He looks dizzy, but he manages to find his bearings and jump safely down from the tube to the finish zone.

"Yes, Ravi!" I shout, jumping and punching the air.

The audience erupts with cheers for Ravi. He made it all the way through the final course, despite the producers' trick. No matter what happens to me, Ravi has a chance to win first place.

As soon as Ravi's off the course, the set hands start to reset it. I watch them all closely, looking for anything out of place. It's surprisingly easy this time. The same set hand who oiled the platform before Ravi's turn is wiping off the platform with her towel. I follow her as she hops down from the platform and toward the dungeon of chains. In one swift movement, she squirts oil onto her hands and glides them down several of the chains. If I hadn't seen her put the oil on her hands, it would look like she was just testing the chains. I memorize which chains she oiled—three different ones next to each other. I will have to skip all three, which means swinging about twelve feet to the next ungreased chain. *I've never made that kind of leap before. Can I do it today?*

"Fiona, you're up," a set hand calls to me. I head toward my start position, but Paul steps in my way. He has a wild look on his face, the kind you have when a loud noise wakes you from a deep sleep.

"Were you telling the truth yesterday?"

"Yes," I say, looking him straight in the eye. He stares back at me then finally steps away so I can pass.

As I walk to my starting line, I hear him say, "Good luck, Fiona."

I turn back to him and smile. "You too, Paul. May the best athlete win."

A minute later, I hear the start horn. I slowly feel my way down the platform toward the wall. Like last time, I manage to climb the wall. Unlike last time, I make it to the top without falling. My biceps are on fire, I'm out of breath, and now I have to make it through the dungeon of chains. I remove my blindfold, take a deep breath, and grab the first chain.

I swing myself steadily from one chain to the next. I loop my feet around the bottom of the chains to create a foothold. This keeps my arms from doing all the work and lets me walk from chain to chain instead of swing. This works until I make it to the middle where I know the next three chains are oiled. I begin to swing all of my body weight, back and forth, as much as possible. I swing, once, twice, three times, then I jump. I fly through the air, arms stretched out. I catch the chain with both hands and hug it tight. *I can't believe I made it past the oil!* But I'm not done yet.

I make it through the dungeon and prepare to jump onto the spinning platform. I've never made it this far, so I can only hope I can do it now. I take a running leap and I jump for the sword. I catch it with my hands. There is no oil on the platform, so my feet don't slip like Ravi's did. I find my balance more easily, but the platform is still spinning. If I'm not careful, I could fall. Slowly I pull the sword from the stone and then time my jump down into the tube.

As soon as I'm inside the dark tube, it pitches forward. The angle is so steep I start to slide down. I can see a familiar pool of sludge below me. I am slipping quickly toward it when the tube lurches backward. Now I'm sliding backward toward the opening on the other end. The tube flings me back and forth twice. I lose my grip again and fall toward the exit. I grasp at the slick walls, but there's nothing to hold on to. I'm falling out of the tube, feet first. At the last moment, I grab the thick rim of the tube. My feet dangle inches above the sludge.

No way am I going back in that mess.

I clutch the rim of the tube and pull my body back into it. Carefully, I turn and jump down safely into the finish zone. The audience explodes with cheers. I hear people chanting my name. I start to get up to my feet, but a wave of nausea hits me. I stay on all fours, hoping it passes. Someone helps me to my feet. I can't look up, I'm too dizzy, but I know it's Sarah by her voice.

"Nice job, Fiona," she says.

I lean myself against her, completely disoriented. Everything is spinning. "I did it," I say, weakly.

"You did. You beat Ravi's time. Too bad we have to penalize you forty points because of your little cheat."

"I didn't cheat!" I shout.

"You skipped three chains. You can't skip obstacles. Those are the rules."

"Whose rules? That bald guy Diego's?"

"The producers' rules, yes. They're the only rules that matter," Sarah snaps. "But your little cheat put you in last place. Paul has to do very poorly for you to come in second. Looks like you're the Loooo-serrrrr."

Sarah walks me to a bench and leaves me with Ravi. He hands me a bottle of water. "You okay?" he asks.

"I'm fine. Just dizzy." My head starts to clear and the full weight of what Sarah said sinks in. "It's over, Ravi. I lost. I'm going to come in last place. We're not going to win."

"You don't know that. I could still win."

"Paul has to fall. If he makes it to the end in a better time than you, he'll outscore us both."

Ravi drapes his arm around my shoulder. "Hey, we did our best. That's all that matters. Now we just have to wait." I lean my head against his shoulder. Slowly the world stops spinning.

We watch the set hands transition the course. We spot the girl wiping off the chains, leaving them clean for Paul. She doesn't add any oil for him. The course will be far easier for Paul than it was for us. He has a clear shot at the win.

The horn blasts for Paul to start. Even blindfolded he makes it up the wall as fast as a squirrel. He slows down on the chains, but eventually he crosses with ease. Unlike last time, Paul jumps high enough to catch the sword and land with his feet squarely on the spinning platform. In half the time it took me to get this far, Paul is already on the final obstacle. He enters the tube. I watch as it rocks back and forth, and I have to look away to keep my nausea from returning. When I glance back, Paul has emerged from the other end of the tube. He stands, firmly gripping the exit opening. All he has to do now is jump down to the finish zone and he's won. But he doesn't jump. He stands in the opening. Seconds pass, then a minute. The audience goes quiet. The announcer whispers into his microphone, "I don't know what's going on. All he has to do is jump. Something's wrong, folks."

Finally, Paul does something. But it's not what anyone expects him to do. Instead of making the easy jump into the finish zone, Paul slides directly down into the pool of muddy sludge water. In this moment, Paul has become the loser. He'll be penalized for not completing the course, for falling before the end. He did what the producers wanted me to do all along. He fell on purpose.

CHAPTER
10

The crowd erupts in murmurs and gasps.
"Oh my goodness," the announcer says,
shocked. "Oh my—I've never seen this. It's
like he just gave up. He won't be in first
place now."

Ravi's eyes meet mine. He has my same
expression of disbelief and growing excitement.
Paul—the golden boy, the one the producers
wanted to win—can't win now. And there's
nothing the producers can do about it.
No matter who wins first place, we beat
the producers. We didn't cheat and we won
anyway. That feels like a victory.

The set hands usher Ravi and me over to the red circle for the awards ceremony. As we cross the sound stage, I see three set hands helping Paul out of the sludge. Cameras descend upon him to capture his low moment.

Eventually, Paul joins me and Ravi in the circle. He's covered in sludge. A wave of sympathy hits me. Yesterday, that was me covered in the gunk. And if Paul is the loser, he will soon be punished with a thick layer of disgusting green slime. "Hey, can I get a towel?" I ask a passing set hand. The set hand shakes his head. *Every set hand in this place carries a towel, and they can't spare one?*

Ravi doesn't ask, he just snatches a towel from the nearest set hand's pocket. "Thanks," he says, sarcastically, then tosses it to Paul.

"Thanks, man," Paul says. I'm surprised to hear that Paul doesn't sound upset. He actually sounds cheerful.

"Paul, why did you do that?" I ask. "You had the win."

He shakes his head. "It wouldn't have been a real win. But if I lost, I knew it would ruin the producers' plan. I decided to cheat the cheaters."

"I'm glad we're finally on the same page," Ravi says, sticking his hand out. Paul shakes it.

Set hands come through to touch up me and Ravi. My hair gets brushed, my face powdered. Ravi's hair gets combed, his shirt straightened. No one touches Paul. The producers must like how bad he looks covered in crud.

The lights dim. The announcer's voice comes on over the speakers. "It's been a long season. We've seen these amazing athletes do amazing things. But there can only be one Ultimate Warrior. In second place, with one thousand, three hundred, and sixty points, the fierce, fearless, and fan favorite, Fiona Chu!" I step out of the circle onto the second place podium. A stagehand places a silver medal around my neck. I made it to second place. I'm proud of my achievements because I earned them. This is why I came here.

"In first place, a warrior who touched our hearts from the very beginning. He's had some ups and downs, but in the end, he showed us what it means to be a true warrior. With a score of one thousand, five hundred, and seventy two points, this year's Ultimate Warrior, and the winner of *Warrior Zone*, is . . . Ravi Murthy!"

The lights swirl, confetti falls, the crowd cheers. From somewhere off to the side, a swarm of people run onto the stage. It's Ravi's family. They've been watching from the audience the whole time! On set, his family covers him in hugs and kisses. Set hands guide Ravi and his family onto the podium. Ravi receives a gold medal and the giant check for thirty thousand dollars.

The lights dim until there's only one spotlight on Paul. He's alone in the loser's circle. He's about to be covered in even more slime and shame, all because he did the right thing. I look over at Ravi, still celebrating with his family. He wouldn't be in first place if it weren't for Paul. Ravi sees me and nods.

"Now, sadly, not everyone can be a winner," the announcer sighs. "One warrior does not get to leave the circle. He's a, say it with me, Looooo-serrrrr."

No, he's not, I think. *Paul isn't a loser. None of us are.*

I step down from my podium and walk back into the circle. Ravi leaves his family and joins the circle too. "What's this?" the announcer says, startled. "Something's happening in the circle. The winners are back. If they're not careful . . . This could get ugly, folks."

I stand beside Paul and I take his arm. Ravi stands on the other side and takes Paul's other arm. The light is low, but I can see Sarah watching from off stage. I look up at the ceiling, past the big tube where, any minute now, slime will come pouring out. Somewhere up there, Diego is in his office with a decision to make. It's up to him if he slimes us. But winners don't get slimed, so if he slimes us, he'll be breaking his own rule. And if he doesn't slime us, it means the loser doesn't get slimed. Also breaking his rule. There's no way he can win. And there's no way we can lose.

"Here it comes, everyone! In three . . . two . . . one!"

Thick, sticky green slime rains down,
drenching the three of us. It oozes into my hair,
down my face. I can feel it between my toes.

"Ooooooh," the audience reacts.

I can see Sarah grinning in the distance.
She thinks she's won. She's wrong. We won.
I smile back at her, then blow kisses to the
crowd. Soon, their winces turn to cheers.
They don't care if we're covered in slime.
I see Sarah's smile fade before she disappears
off stage.

Ravi, Paul, and I hug and high five. Ravi's
family runs into the circle and joins our
celebration. We may be covered in slime, but
we aren't cheaters. There are no losers today—
just three unbeatable athletes.

MASON FALLS MYSTERIES

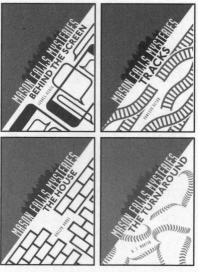

EVEN AN ORDINARY TOWN HAS ITS SECRETS.